CLEVER
• Publishing •

Text copyright © 2021 by **Elena Ulyeva**
Illustrations copyright © 2021 by **Daria Parkhaeva**

First published in the United States of America in May 2022 by "Clever-Media-Group" LLC
www.clever-publishing.com

ISBN 978-1-954738-42-3 (hardcover)

For information about permission to reproduce selections from this book, write to:
CLEVER PUBLISHING
79 MADISON AVENUE; 8TH FLOOR
NEW YORK, NY 10016

For general inquiries, contact: info@clever-publishing.com
CLEVER is a registered trademark of "Clever-Media-Group" LLC

To place an order for Clever Publishing books, please contact The Quarto Group:
sales@quarto.com • Tel: (+1) 800-328-0590

Art created digitally
Book design by Michelle Martinez
MANUFACTURED, PRINTED, AND ASSEMBLED IN CHINA

10 9 8 7 6 5 4 3 2 1

HEDGEHOG'S
HOME FOR
SUMMER

by
ELENA ULYEVA

illustrated by
DARIA PARKHAEVA

2

One day, Hedgehog was walking in the forest when he saw that all of his friends were so happy.

It was finally **summertime**, and everyone had received a special gift from summer.

"**How wonderful!**" Hedgehog exclaimed. He hoped that summer had brought a gift for him, too.

I wonder what it could be!

"**Summer** has brought us the bright, hot sun!" cheered the flowers when they saw Hedgehog.

Buzz!

"Our leaves **grow**,
and our petals open."

Sniff!

Buzz!

Yum!

"And summer gave us **flowers**,"
sang the butterflies and bumblebees.

"We love the **sweet** nectar."

Buzz!

"Summer has brought me soft, green grass," Rabbit giggled. "It feels so nice on my paws. Come on, Fox, let's play!"

Boing!

"We have warm water," the frogs croaked. "It's perfect for us!"

Ribbit!

Splash!

Quack!

"We love it, too!" called the ducks and the fish.
"Come and join us, Hedgehog!"

Hedgehog wanted to go in the water, but he didn't know how to swim. So he explored the plants near the pond instead.

"Thanks anyway!"
said Hedgehog.
"Have fun!"

"Hello, birds!" called Hedgehog. "What gifts did summer bring to you?"

"I have been given the gift of my chicks," Mama Bird chirped. "Yesterday, there were eggs in the nest, and today, there are baby birds!"

Chirp!

Chirp!

Hedgehog found some other forest friends while looking for flowers.

"What do you have there?"

he asked.

14

"**Nuts** and **corn** and all kinds of **delicious foods!**" cried Gopher and Hamster.

"**Me, too!**" called Mouse.
"Summer has brought a nut for me!"

Hedgehog didn't want nuts or corn, so he kept looking for his gift from summer.

He soon found some raspberry bushes. The berries looked very tasty.

"Is this my special gift from summer?" he wondered.

"Raspberries are the BEST gift," cheered Bear. "Nothing is sweeter or tastier! Look at all of the berries that summer has brought me!"

Buzz!

Buzz!

Sniffle!
Sniffle!

Hedgehog sat down on a tree stump. "Everyone has gotten a gift from summer except me," he sniffed. "I think summer forgot about me."

Just then, Owl saw Hedgehog crying and flew over to him.

"What's wrong, Hedgehog?" Owl asked.

"Oh, Owl, everyone has gotten a special gift from summer except me," sighed Hedgehog.

"The flowers got the sun. The butterflies and bees have the flowers. Rabbit and Fox have the soft grass.

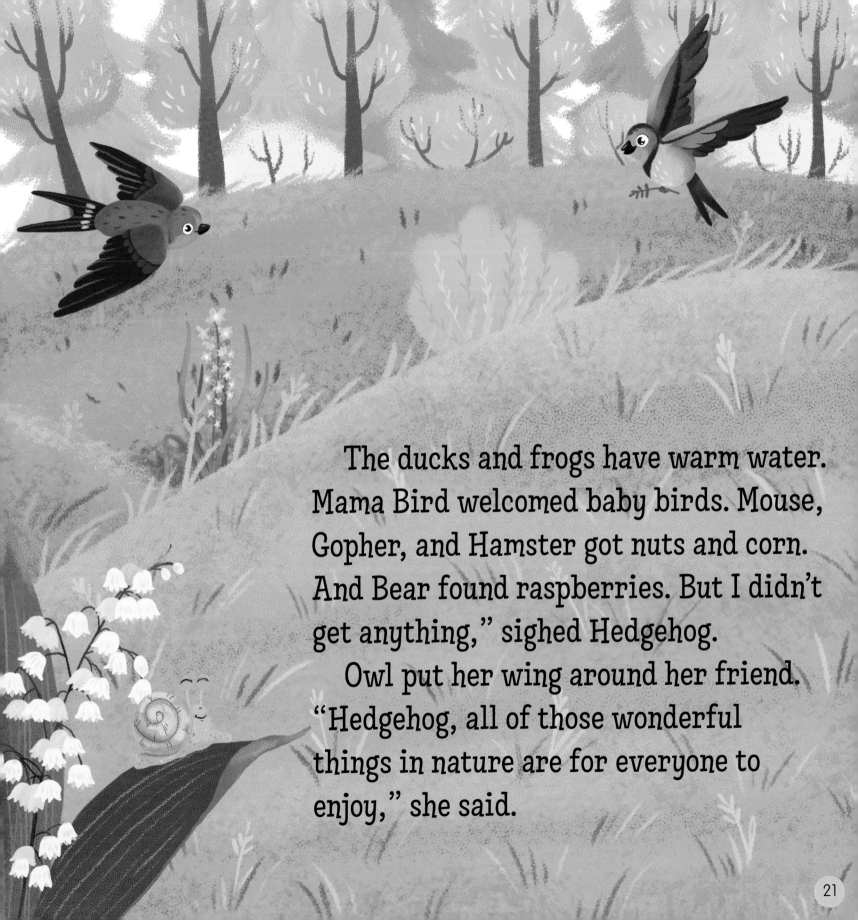

The ducks and frogs have warm water. Mama Bird welcomed baby birds. Mouse, Gopher, and Hamster got nuts and corn. And Bear found raspberries. But I didn't get anything," sighed Hedgehog.

Owl put her wing around her friend. "Hedgehog, all of those wonderful things in nature are for everyone to enjoy," she said.

Hedgehog thought about
what Owl had told him.
He smiled knowing that
he, too, was given
the warm sun, soft
grass, and delicious
food as a gift from summer.

Suddenly, something dropped to the ground in front of him. It was a shiny red apple! And it looked delicious!

"My gift!" Hedgehog exclaimed. "Summer didn't forget about me after all!"

23

Hedgehog took a big bite of his apple.
It was crispy, juicy, and delicious.

"Thank you summer.
This is the best gift,"
he said.

"I love summer!"

Hedgehog exclaimed.

Buzz!

He smiled and breathed
in the sweet smells
of the fresh grass
and blooming flowers.

Buzz!

"Wow," said Hedgehog.
"All of my friends are having
fun and enjoying summer.

Nature has taken care of everything for us!"

LET'S LEARN ABOUT SUMMER WITH HEDGEHOG!

SUMMER MONTHS

JUNE

Flowers and trees continue to bloom and grow. Everyone celebrates the warm sunshine and blue skies.

JULY

The hot sun warms the land and water. The days get longer, and many people like to spend time outside.

AUGUST

Gifts from Nature—like berries and nuts—are ready to be picked. The sun still shines brightly. Thunderstorms happen more often.

WHAT HAPPENS IN SUMMER?

THE SUN WARMS

WARM WINDS BLOW

RAIN FALLS

THUNDERSTORMS FILL THE SKY

TEMPERATURES RISE

RAINBOWS APPEAR IN SUN AND RAIN

31

How to Make
HOMEMADE BUBBLES

What You Need

- Large plastic bowl with lid
- Measuring cups
- 6 cups water
- 1 cup dish soap*
- Mixing spoon
- ¼ cup light corn syrup**
- Large baking sheet
- Homemade bubble wand (see instructions)

*Regular dish soap (not Ultra) works best.
**If you're using Ultra dish soap, double the amount of corn syrup.

Homemade Bubble Wand

Thread a length of yarn through one drinking straw, and then through a second drinking straw. Tie the ends of the yarn together. Dip your wand into the bubble solution.

What You Do

Pour the water into the plastic bowl, then add the dish soap and slowly stir until the soap is mixed in. Try not to let foam or bubbles form while you stir. Add the corn syrup and stir until combined. You can use the solution right away, but to make even better bubbles, put the lid on the container and let your bubble solution sit overnight. When you're ready to use, carefully pour it onto the large baking sheet. Dip your bubble wand into the mixture, slowly pull it out, wait a few seconds, and then wave the wand around.